Hansel, Gretel, and the Ugly Duckling

Crabtree Publishing Company

www.crabtreebooks.com
1-800-387-7650

PMB 59051,
350 Fifth Ave., 59th Floor
New York, NY 10118

616 Welland Ave.
St. Catharines, ON
L2M 5V6

Published by Crabtree Publishing in 2013

For Benjamin

Series editor: Louise John
Series Design: Emil Dacanay
Design: Lisa Peacock
Consultant: Shirley Bickler
Editor: Kathy Middleton
Proofreaders: Kelly McNiven, Crystal Sikkens
Notes to adults: Reagan Miller
Print and production coordinator: Katherine Berti

Text © Hilary Robinson 2013
Illustration © Simona Sanfilippo 2013

Printed in Canada/022013/BF20130114

First published in 2013 by Wayland
(A division of Hachette Children's Books)

Library and Archives Canada Cataloguing in Publication

Robinson, Hilary, 1962-
     Hansel, Gretel, and the ugly duckling / written by Hilary Robinson ; illustrated by Simona Sanfilippo.

(Tadpoles: fairytale jumbles)
Issued also in electronic format.
ISBN 978-0-7787-1157-5 (bound).
--ISBN 978-0-7787-1166-7 (pbk.)

     I. Sanfilippo, Simona II. Title. III. Series: Tadpoles (St. Catharines, Ont.). Fairytale jumbles

PZ7.R6235Ha 2013   j823'.914   C2012-908164-7

Library of Congress Cataloging-in-Publication Data

Robinson, Hilary, 1962-
  Hansel, Gretel, and the ugly duckling / by Hilary Robinson ; illustrated by Simona Sanfilippo.
     pages cm. -- (Tadpoles: fairytale jumbles)
     Summary: The ugly duckling comes to the rescue when two siblings become trapped in a wicked old lady's cottage.
     ISBN 978-0-7787-1157-5 (reinforced library binding : alk. paper) -- ISBN 978-0-7787-1166-7 (pbk. : alk. paper) -- ISBN 978-1-4271-9305-6 (electronic pdf) -- ISBN 978-1-4271-9229-5 (electronic html)
     [1. Stories in rhyme. 2. Characters in literature--Fiction. 3. Rescues--Fiction.] I. Sanfilippo, Simona, illustrator. II. Title.

     PZ8.3.R575Han 2013
     [E]--dc23
                                        2012047908

Hansel, Gretel, and the Ugly Duckling

Written by Hilary Robinson
Illustrated by Simona Sanfilippo

Crabtree Publishing Company

www.crabtreebooks.com

"Hansel," said Gretel, "we have no food, and Dad needs more wood to make pegs. Let's walk to the farm down by the stream, and sell what we have for some eggs."

"We'll go through the forest," said Hansel, "and pick up some wood on the way. We'll buy some wheat to grind into flour and be back by the end of the day."

Hansel dropped stones to make a long trail so they could find their way back.

Just as they got to the farm by the stream,
they heard a little duck quack.

"Oh no!" cried Gretel. "Look at those ducks!
They're teasing the one that is brown.
They think he's not as handsome as them
and the ugliest duck in the town!"

10

"Look how they leave him only the crusts,
while they eat the bread that is white.
And look how they snuggle up in the reeds,
while he sleeps alone through the night."

They bought the grain and collected the wood, then baked some bread for their breakfast.

Father said, "Children, I need some woodchips.
Can you gather some up in the forest?"

This time they took bread for the ducks
and left a crumb trail as their guide.

But nighttime soon came
and the children got lost.
"Where will we sleep?" they both cried.

"Look over there in the trees," Hansel said.
"That house! It is ever so sweet!

Do we dare go and knock on the door
and ask for something to eat?"

Just at that moment a woman appeared.
"Ha, ha!" she said. "Come with me!"

But as they stepped in through the door, she locked it and threw out the key.

The little duck had followed the trail
and eaten the bread as he ran.
He saw the children trapped in the house,
and the clever duck thought up a plan.

When the old lady went to bed,
he picked up the key for the door.
He flapped his wings, flew up in the air,
and dropped it right on the floor.

"Hansel," said Gretel, "the duckling is here!
I can't believe what he's done!
He brought us the key to help us get out.
Unlock the door and let's run!"

The children ran far away from the house,
with the duckling leading them on.
He lived the rest of his days on their pond
and grew into a...

...beautiful swan!

Notes for Adults

Tadpoles: Fairytale Jumbles are designed for transitional and early fluent readers. The books may also be used for a read-aloud or shared reading with younger children. **Tadpoles: Fairytale Jumbles** are humorous stories with a unique twist on traditional fairytales. Each story can be compared to the original fairytale, or appreciated on its own. Fairytales are a key type of literary text found in the Common Core State Standards.

THE FOLLOWING BEFORE, DURING, AND AFTER READING ACTIVITY SUGGESTIONS SUPPORT LITERACY SKILL DEVELOPMENT AND CAN ENRICH SHARED READING EXPERIENCES:

1. Make reading fun! Choose a time to read when you and the child are relaxed and have time to share the story.

2. Before reading, invite the child to preview the book. The child can read the title, look at the illustrations, skim through the text, and make predictions as to what will happen in the story. Predicting sets a clear purpose for reading and learning.

3. During reading, encourage the child to monitor his or her understanding by asking questions to draw conclusions, making connections, and using context clues to understand unfamiliar words.

4. After reading, ask the child to review his or her predictions. Were they correct? Discuss different parts of the story, including main characters, setting, main events, and the problem and solution. If the child is familiar with the original fairytale, invite he or she to identify the similarities and differences between the two versions of the story.

5. Encourage the child to use his or her imagination to create fairytale jumbles based on other familiar stories.

6. Give praise! Children learn best in a positive environment.

IF YOU ENJOYED THIS BOOK, WHY NOT TRY ANOTHER TADPOLES: FAIRYTALE JUMBLES STORY?

Goldilocks and the Wolf	978-0-7787-8023-6 RLB	978-0-7787-8034-2 PB
	978-1-4271-9156-4 Ebook (HTML)	978-1-4271-9148-9 Ebook (PDF)
Snow White and the Enormous Turnip	978-0-7787-8024-3 RLB	978-0-7787-8035-9 PB
	978-1-4271-9158-8 Ebook (HTML)	978-1-4271-9150-2 Ebook (PDF)
The Elves and the Emperor	978-0-7787-8025-0 RLB	978-0-7787-8036-6 PB
	978-1-4271-9159-5 Ebook (HTML)	978-1-4271-9151-9 Ebook (PDF)
Three Pigs and a Gingerbread Man	978-0-7787-8026-7 RLB	978-0-7787-8037-3 PB
	978-1-4271-9157-1 Ebook (HTML)	978-1-4271-9149-6 Ebook (PDF)
Rapunzel and the Billy Goats	978-0-7787-1154-4 RLB	978-0-7787-1158-2 PB
	978-1-4271-9226-4 Ebook (HTML)	978-1-4271-9302-5 Ebook (PDF)
Beauty and the Pea	978-0-7787-1155-1 RLB	978-0-7787-1159-9 PB
	978-1-4271-9227-1 Ebook (HTML)	978-1-4271-9303-2 Ebook (PDF)
Cinderella and the Beanstalk	978-0-7787-1156-8 RLB	978-0-7787-1161-2 PB
	978-1-4271-9228-8 Ebook (HTML)	978-1-4271-9304-9 Ebook (PDF)

VISIT WWW.CRABTREEBOOKS.COM FOR OTHER CRABTREE BOOKS.